WITHDRAWN
Final Crossing

Sean Rodman

orca soundings

ORCA BOOK PUBLISHERS

Copyright © 2014 Sean Rodman

Library and Archives Canada Cataloguing in Publication

Rodman, Sean, 1972-, author
Final crossing / Sean Rodman.
(Orca soundings)

Issued in print and electronic formats.
ISBN 978-1-4598-0558-3 (bound).--ISBN 978-1-4598-0552-1 (pbk.).--
ISBN 978-1-4598-0553-8 (pdf).--ISBN 978-1-4598-0554-5 (epub)

I. Title. II. Series: Orca soundings
PS8635.O355F56 2014   jc813'.6   C2013-906736-1
C2013-906737-X

First published in the United States, 2014
Library of Congress Control Number: 2013954151

Summary: Will and Big O are brothers, on the run and trying to stay together.
Breaking into cars for small change, they stumble across a kidnap victim and
end up in a fight for their lives.

MIX
Paper from
responsible sources
FSC® C016245
www.fsc.org

*Orca Book Publishers is dedicated to preserving the environment and has
printed this book on Forest Stewardship Council® certified paper.*

Orca Book Publishers gratefully acknowledges the support for its publishing
programs provided by the following agencies: the Government of Canada through
the Canada Book Fund and the Canada Council for the Arts,
and the Province of British Columbia through the BC Arts Council
and the Book Publishing Tax Credit.

Cover image by iStockphoto.com

ORCA BOOK PUBLISHERS
PO Box 5626, Stn. B
Victoria, BC Canada
v8R 6s4

ORCA BOOK PUBLISHERS
PO Box 468
Custer, WA USA
98240-0468

www.orcabook.com
Printed and bound in Canada.

17 16 15 14 • 4 3 2 1

For my sister,
who started this journey for me

Chapter One

Like most of my brother's plans, this one is stupid and illegal.

And I'm going through with it. Like I always do.

Big O squints through the rain-spattered windshield of our old Ford pickup. Cars are lining up to be fed into the belly of a big ferry that looms in the evening twilight over the dock.

"What I'm saying is, it's a long ride from here to Seattle. And we could use a little entertainment." Big O shoves the pickup into gear and nudges it forward.

"You want entertainment, you could read a newspaper," I say.

Big O shoots me a quick look, like he doesn't appreciate me being unreasonable.

I shrug. "What? You like the comics, right?"

"You're supposed to be the smart one. So stay with me here and do the math," he continues. "There's what, like, four hundred cars on this ferry. We've got two hours. We wait until everybody goes upstairs, leaves their cars behind. Then we take a little walk. Figure out who's left us a present in their car." As he speaks, Big O carefully steers us up the loading ramp into the ferry. Following the directions of a guy in a blue uniform with an orange flashlight, he pulls right up to the SUV in front of us.

"So nobody's going to notice us taking their stuff?" I say.

Big O kills the engine. "I'll stand lookout. You're awesome at boosting windows and doors." There he goes, trying to butter me up. "Look, it's a simple plan. And it doesn't break any of your rules."

Being the brains of our operation, I had set a couple of ground rules for our partnership. One, nobody gets hurt. That's how Dad went down. Two, no drugs. Duh. And three, never steal anything so big that it'll attract attention. I unbuckle my seat belt so I can swivel on the vinyl seat to face him. My older brother, Big O, is chubby. Not fat but baby-faced, people call it. Although he tends to smack them if they say it to his face. That layer of fat hides some pretty solid muscle.

Me, I'm the opposite. Thin. Messy brown hair. Like a ferret with glasses. But we both have the same sneaky blue eyes. A little shifty, like our dad.

"Okay, it's not the worst plan ever," I say. It is, in fact, a terrible plan. But I don't want to hurt his feelings, so I need to break this gently. "There's a lot of things I like about it."

O nods enthusiastically, his Oakland A's ballcap bobbing up and down.

"But here's a problem," I continue. "This ferry is basically a giant floating box. If we get caught, and we're in the middle of the friggin' ocean, where do we run?"

But O is ready for this one. He smiles serenely, like an evil version of one of those little Buddha statues.

"Will, open your mind to the possibilities." Big O reaches over, puts one arm on my shoulder and, with the other, gestures to the rows and rows of cars now parked in front of us. Like a herd of cows, people are already leaving their cars behind and heading for the stairs to the upper deck.

"Where do we run? That's only a problem," drawls O, "if we get caught. So let's not do that this time, all right?"

I rub my face, thinking it through. The real problem, when you get right down to it, is money. Even if we sleep in the truck, we'll need some money for food and gas.

"How much cash have you got left?" I ask O.

He pulls out a brown leather wallet, white and worn on the edges. He opens it up wide to show me a couple of quarters. I snort. I have a few bucks. Maybe enough for a coffee or two. Everything else, we blew on the ferry ticket.

Maybe Big O is right. If we're careful, maybe his plan will work.

"Okay," I say. "Let's do it."

Big O shakes both fists in the air like he's just scored a touchdown. "That's one for me!"

"But," I continue, "I'm adding a couple more rules."

"Seriously, man?" Big O says, fists dropping to his sides. "You are the most uptight criminal. Ever."

"We do this, it's by my rules," I say, crossing my arms. "Take it or leave it."

Big O heaves a sigh, like this is killing him. "Fine, whatever. What are the rules?"

"First, we're going to take cash only. We look for jackets, purses, whatever. We don't take anything we have to sell."

Big O nods reasonably.

"Second, I figure we need about a hundred bucks to get us to Uncle Steve's. So once we get that much, we stop."

Now O looks less certain. He shifts his big frame in the driver's seat.

"What if it's something really nice?" he says.

"Like what?" I ask.

"Like...like a gold ring."

"What are you," I say, "a pirate? Why would someone leave a gold ring in their car? You're an idiot."

Big O punches my arm. "No, you're the idiot," he mutters. "You'd leave a perfectly good gold ring behind."

"Moving on," I say loudly, "third and final rule. You're the lookout, so I'm the only one going into the car. You keep your eyes up at all times. If there's any chance of us being seen, we don't do it. And if something goes wrong, if we get split up, then we meet—I dunno, at the cafeteria."

Big O fiddles with the gearshift for a moment, thinking it through. Then he holds out his hand for a high five. I slap it.

"Y'know, we make a great team. Like Ben and Jerry," Big O says as he opens his door. "Or wait—Bert and Ernie? Which ones are the puppets?"

I rub my face again. This is going to be a long night.

Chapter Two

The two of us are walking a couple of cars apart, trying to look casual. I can feel the rumbling of the ferry's engines through the deck as it makes its way out of the port. Pretty much everyone has cleared out of the car deck now, drawn to the upper deck by the lure of fried food in the cafeteria. There are still a few people sleeping in their cars, which makes me nervous.

We continue to walk forward, scanning left and right. Big O is looking for trouble while I'm looking for targets.

I think the key to being a successful small-time crook is setting out some rules for yourself. I'm a rules guy. Which seems a little ironic given my current occupation, which involves breaking a lot of rules.

Rule number one is knowing your limitations. For example, I walk right by a shiny black Audi. It's new, beautiful and probably loaded with all sorts of goodies inside. But it's likely also loaded with a state-of-the-art alarm. Movement sensors and a computer brain that will figure out what I'm doing as I try to open the door. And the car is smart enough to call its owner. Or the cops. Nope, I'm moving on.

Next up, a minivan. Two car seats in the back, colorful kids' stuff scattered about. A shapeless purple purse lying on the passenger seat. I pause for a moment, thinking about rule number two—weigh the costs and benefits. The costs? It's a relatively new model of vehicle—nothing like that Audi, but it might still take a little time to get into. The benefits? That purse could contain some cash. I study the purse, trying to figure out what the lumps inside might be. You know what? I bet it just has a bunch of spare diapers, wipes and soothers. Moving on.

Finally, something I can work with. A big Toyota sedan, about fifteen years old but in great condition. Veteran's license plates. A stack of CDs under the stereo. And a suit jacket lying neatly across the back seat. Bingo. This is clearly an old man's car. Old guys like to keep cash around and tend to forget where they put it. The car is ancient enough to have locks I can deal with and no security system.

I give a low whistle to Big O. He holds up, then comes back to the driver's side of the Toyota. He pulls out his cell phone and pretends to be talking into it while he rotates around. Keeping a lookout.

Lockpicking was always a thing with me. When I was a toddler, Dad let me play with his practice locks in the workshop, the ones he used to sharpen his skills. By the time I was ten, I was getting pretty good and had made my own lockpick set. Hey, some kids are good at soccer or video games. Everybody has to have a hobby. It was just that mine was illegal.

Locks on automobiles are a whole different breed from your average house lock. Some special tools are required. I stay on the passenger side and consider my options. I have a slim jim tucked into the lining of my jacket. It's a long, thin piece of metal with a notch at the end.

Same thing a mechanic might use to get into your mom's car if she locked herself out. Slide the slim jim down the side of the window. Fish around until you catch the lock mechanism, then pull up hard. It works, but it can take a little while and you look pretty suspicious while you're at it. So instead, my first choice is always my tryout keys.

Dad left these babies behind along with some other tools I scooped up before we got moved into a foster home. I pull them out and flip through the set. They look pretty much like an ordinary set of car keys on a ring, nothing special. Except that each key is designed as sort of a "master key" for particular models of cars. They're meant to be used by auto mechanics and car dealers but occasionally fall into the wrong hands. Like mine.

I select one that has worked on other Toyotas and slide it into the lock.

Gently rocking the key up and down, I jiggle it for a minute until I feel the lock give. I turn firmly, and there's a satisfying clunk as the lock pops open.

Quickly, I open the door and slide over to unlock the driver's side. Big O squeezes in.

"I'd give that an eight out of ten," he says. "Good form, but a little slow."

"I'll never make the Olympics, coach." I reach back and hand him the suit jacket. "Check that out while I do the rest." Working efficiently, I go through all the compartments and pocket anything valuable.

"Cha-ching," says Big O. He pulls a twenty-dollar bill from the jacket. I close the glove compartment after scooping up a couple of loose quarters.

"We're outta here." I start to get out, but Big O doesn't move. Instead, he pulls out the CDs from the shelf under the car stereo. Not this again.

"Aw, come on. We don't need any CDs. Let's go."

"I'm sick of all our tunes," he says, like it's obvious. I sigh heavily, but I don't freak out. I've seen this before. Big O likes his music. He can be a real snob about it, but I have to admit, he does know his stuff. From jazz to hip-hop, the guy is a walking Wikipedia of songs.

"Most of this is crap," he says darkly, nearing the end of the pile. Then he brightens. "This'll do—Muddy Waters. Some righteous blues." Big O flips over the CD and starts to read the cover. "You know, the Rolling Stones ripped off Muddy Waters in a big way."

"Focus, dude." I reach over and snatch the CD from him. "Moving on."

He sighs at my lack of interest, then grabs the CD back and pockets it. At the same time, we both get out of the Toyota, carefully locking and closing the doors behind us. Don't want to draw attention to ourselves.

Too late.

"Hey!" It's one of the crew, dark blue coveralls and a bright orange traffic vest. He's walking up the alley between the cars toward us. I stare hard at Big O, hoping he can read my mind. *Don't freaking panic. Don't run, because there's nowhere to run to. We have to bluff our way through this.*

I lean in to look at the guy's name tag. "What seems to be the problem, Mr.—uh—Dorkney?" I say, friendly as hell. Too friendly—he looks at me a little strangely.

"Everybody needs to get above decks," Dorkney says firmly. "We're going to be in open water soon, and there's some heavy weather. It's regulation that you can't stay with the vehicles down here." He gestures toward the car we just got out of. "You have everything

16

you need from your car? Might be a while."

Big O clears his throat. "From our car? Yeah. We were just getting a couple of things to take with us. We'll head right up." I nod enthusiastically. We walk in the opposite direction of the crewman as he raps on the window of another car to wake someone up.

I don't say anything until we're headed up the stairwell. Our feet clank on the metal steps.

"You thinking what I'm thinking?" I say quietly.

"That my great idea was worth about twenty bucks," says Big O. "Crappy luck, huh?"

"No, no. Might be pretty good luck, actually." I pull Big O to one side of the corridor, letting a mother cradling a baby walk past. "Now the crew is making sure nobody will be down there. As long as we're careful, the car deck is ours for the taking." Big O pulls off his ballcap and wipes a hand through greasy hair. And smiles his evil Buddha smile.

We wait, watching the dark ocean outside the windows and feeling the ferry shudder each time a big wave breaks over the bow. Finally, Big O can't stand it anymore, and I'm pretty sure no one is watching. We slip back down the stairwell.

Chapter Three

I lose count of how many cars we go through in the next half hour. Pick a target, jiggle the tryout keys, pop the lock, raid the inside. Big O and I get into a rhythm, and it feels good. There are a few hiccups. I nearly snap one of the tryout keys because I'm rushing. We have to slide behind a big truck when two crew members walk by, talking loudly about union wages. But for the most part, it's smooth.

After a while, we end up crouched beside the tire of a big SUV. Big O's face is red, and he's sweating.

"What have you got?" he says quietly.

I pull a handful of bills and change from my pocket and start counting. He does the same.

"Forty-five bucks and some coin. You?"

"Forty-two," Big O says, passing the money over to me. "Still short."

"Close enough to one hundred," I say and slide our combined money into my wallet. "Let's call it a night."

"You always were a quitter," Big O says. He's half-joking. "You said one hundred dollars. One more car and we're done. There's got to be something easy around here."

He stands up and looks quickly left and right. He looks like a prairie dog with bad intentions, beady eyes jerkily scanning the deck for a target. Finally, Big O sees something he likes and drops down next to me again.

"Got it. Old Ford van. Something from the eighties. Looks like a piece of cake."

I puff out my cheeks and shake my head. "I dunno. We're pushing our luck."

Big O looks at me and slowly lifts one eyebrow. "Quitter."

"All right, all right," I say. "I'll take a look." We quickly duckwalk along, Big O in the lead. Staying low and weaving between the cars. The ferry is starting to really rock in the storm. It's not so bad that we can't move around, but some of the cars are shifting noisily on their suspensions. I can hear the dull roar of the waves hitting the bow of the ship.

"This one," whispers Big O. He jerks his thumb at the van looming over us. "See? Piece of cake."

"Piece of crap, actually," I mutter. It's an Econoline van. Big and boxy. Originally blue but now decorated with orange patches of rust around the wheel wells and doors. No windows in the back, just siding with faded letters advertising *Speedy Mechanical Repairs*. Big O is right about one thing—it should be easy to get into. Maybe a few dollars in the glove compartment. If we're lucky and the owner is a contractor, maybe he keeps some serious cash on hand.

"All right," I say quietly. "Keep an eye out." I creep around to the side of the van, leaving Big O peering over the tops of the cars around us. Pulling out my tryout keys, I select one and slide it into the lock. I'm about to start jiggling the key when I hear a muffled thump.

From inside the van.

I freeze, straining to hear it again. Waves. Creaking. Wind. Big O appears around the corner.

"What's the holdup?"

"I thought I heard something. Like, from inside," I say. "Dog, maybe?"

"Don't want that," Big O says quietly, then snorts a laugh. "You remember the Chihuahua in the Jaguar? Sleeping behind the backseat, right? You came flying out of the car, and I swear, the dog's teeth were longer than its body. Hilarious, totally—"

I cut him off with a gesture and put my ear against the cold steel side of the van. "Let me listen for a second."

Seconds tick by. Nothing. All I hear is my own blood pumping in my ears. My armpits feel sticky with sweat, and my fingers ache a little as I start with the tryout keys again. "Okay, I'm going to get this over with."

I work one tryout key after another, shaking and twisting each one in the lock. Finally, I feel a solid click. The lock gives a little—then pops open. I grab the silver door handle above it and pull. With a rusty grinding sound, the door opens. Big O smiles and slaps my back.

"Let's get in there and get paid."

I slip into the interior, then reach over to unlock the passenger door for Big O. The windows are so dirty, not much light is getting through, and it takes a second for my eyes to adjust to the dimness. The floor is littered with old fast-food wrappers and cups. Big O flips open the glove compartment and retrieves a handful of CDs. I shake my head. Man, he's obsessed with his tunes today. Then I look into the back of the van.

It's lined with two metal shelving units. Shadowy shapes are scattered across the shelves, and a big pile of tarps is crumpled on the floor. More fast-food wrappers have tumbled into the far corner.

"This is worse than my old room," I say. Crinkling my nose against the smell,

I work my way out of the driver's seat and shuffle into the back of the van.

"*Your power within! Change your thoughts, change your life!*" Big O says loudly, then starts laughing to himself.

I stop. "What the hell? Keep it down!"

"Dude who owns the van seems to be into self-help in a big way. All of these CDs are like that—*101 Habits of Powerful People, Make Yourself Better Every Day.* Waste of my time." I hear the clatter of plastic cases as he tosses the CDs back into the glove compartment in disgust.

"This waste of time was your idea," I mutter and start to search through the clutter on the shelves. Then my foot catches on the pile of blue plastic tarps and I sprawl forward, landing heavily.

Something grunts. Under the plastic sheets.

My first thought is that it's another Chihuahua situation. I scramble to my feet, ready to run. But then I hear the sound again, and it doesn't sound like a dog. There's something about the noise that makes me carefully peel back one edge of a plastic sheet.

Something small in there. I lean in close, trying to figure out what I'm looking at in the half-light. It takes a minute. Then, like a camera snapping into focus, I see her.

It's a girl. My age. Long blond hair in a ponytail. Rag tied around her mouth.

And panic in her eyes.

Chapter Four

"Don't tell me," says Big O from the front. "You found some more self-help CDs back there."

"Not exactly," I say and start pulling back the tarp. As I'm doing this, the girl is wriggling on the floor and grunting. Her hands are tied together with silver duct tape. Same thing with her feet. She's frantic, and I'm freaked out. I start making shushing noises, like she's an upset baby or something. That seems to make her madder.

"Holy crap!" Big O crouches beside me. "What's she doing hiding under the tarps?"

"She wasn't hiding."

The girl keeps shaking her head, trying to get rid of the red rag that's gagging her. I reach out to untie it, and she calms down. I pull it away, and she starts coughing and making croaking noises. Big O grabs my shoulder and pulls me back to him.

"She is bad news, man. We don't want any part of this," he whispers.

"She can hear you, dude," I say.

Big O hesitates, looking down at the girl on the floor.

"You seriously saying that we leave her here?" I say.

"I'm just saying she's not our problem. Let's cut her loose and then get out."

The girl stops coughing and looks at us. She tries to say something, but no words come out. It looks like it hurts her to try and talk.

"We can't just walk away," I say.

"No, but we bring her to the cops, and what happens to us?" Big O shakes his head. "They're not going to give us a medal for breaking into a bunch of cars and then finding— this." He motions vaguely at the girl. "They'll ask a lot of questions, then put the cuffs on us. And who knows what's going on here? Maybe she's a biker's girlfriend or something and this is part of a gang war."

We both look down at the girl.

"She looks too nice for something like that," I say. "She's not a biker chick."

"How can you tell?"

"She's got a nice haircut. Plus, those jeans are really expensive, I think. She's rich."

"You think? How can you tell?" says Big O, intrigued. "How much are the shoes worth?"

"What, now I'm a fashion expert? I'm just saying—"

Before I can answer, the girl coughs again, then speaks in a gravelly voice.

"He's coming back," she rasps and holds up her bound hands. "Please."

Screw it.

"Give me your knife," I say to Big O. He frowns, but pulls a battered jack-knife out of his pocket and hands it over. I saw away at the duct tape around her feet. It feels like ages before the tape frays, then snaps apart. The girl slowly sits up, wincing. She must have been tied up for a long time. She tries to say something again, fails and licks her cracked lips. I lean in close.

"Run," she says. "Now."

And right on cue, we hear the rattle of keys in the door. Driver's side. A tall shadow on the glass.

I grab the girl by one arm and haul her backward. Big O slams the rear doors open and we all tumble onto the deck. Big O is off like a rocket, sprinting away between the cars. The girl tries to run but stumbles immediately and falls onto her knees. I reach down and drag her after me as fast as I can. If I dropped her and ran, I'd be long gone, just like Big O. But after being tied up for so long, the girl can't walk, and I can't leave her. Whoever the bad guy is, he's going to be on top of us any second. I can almost feel a hand on my back when I see Big O again. He's crouched beside a silver minivan, waiting for us. He points under the minivan and we all scramble underneath. I try to breathe through my nose and keep quiet.

Hoping the man following us can't hear my heart slamming away inside my chest.

I've ended up lying next to the girl, her face turned toward me. Just a couple of inches away. I can't help but notice how pretty she is. I mean, she's got a big grease mark on her cheek and looks pretty freaked out. But her eyes are a nice dark blue, like the deep end of a calm swimming pool.

She looks at me, silently. Then we both hear a voice, over the wind cutting through the deck, over the creaking of the cars.

"Marissa?" His deep voice gets louder, and I can see a pair of shiny black dress shoes right in front of us. Walking past slowly.

"Marissa? I understand why you ran. I do. But it's not what you think. Come back—everything will be fine." His voice goes from sweet to knife-sharp as he says quietly, "Dammit." He calls her name again and again as he heads across the car deck, his voice finally fading out.

"That's you?" I whisper to the girl. "Marissa?"

She nods but doesn't say anything, just holds a finger to her lips. Shushing me.

"I think he's gone," I finally whisper. "Who was that?"

Chapter Five

"He called himself Mr. Blank." Her voice still sounds rough as she whispers. "I never saw him before tonight. I was on the way home from my friend's. About a block away, a van pulls over and that guy steps out. I froze up. It was so fast. He just grabbed me, hauled me into the van and tied me up. Told me that if I didn't cause any trouble, I would be fine."

"So he was a psycho killer?" says Big O on the other side of her. I'm not sure what's appropriate in this particular social situation. But I'm sure that Big O is being inappropriate. The guy has no manners.

"You don't have to answer that," I say.

"No, it wasn't like that. It was a kidnapping. He took a picture of me, told me that my parents would pay up. Or he'd make sure that they would never find me."

"That's terrible," I say.

"Yeah. It could have been. But then you guys showed up. I'd still be in that van if it weren't for you."

In the dark, she can't see me blush. I hope. "No big deal."

"How did you know I was in there, anyway?"

Big O blows a breath out between pursed lips. "That's an interesting story."

"We were just lucky," I say, trying to sound smooth. "I was walking by and I heard some noises inside the van."

"Then we tried the door and it was open." Big O continues the lie. "And there you were."

"Well, thank you." Marissa peers out from under the van. "So, are we on a ferry? Where's it going?"

Of course—she has no idea where Mr. Blank was taking her. I explain about the ferry, that it has about an hour to go before we land on the other side. She thinks for a minute, then starts squirming out from underneath the van.

"We'd better go."

"Wait, where are you going?" I say.

"Upstairs. I need to find some cops or something."

I wriggle out too. Big O is a little slower off the mark—Marissa and I are crouched by the van while he's still flopping around underneath, trying to get unstuck.

"But the kidnapper—he might see you," I say to her.

"I can't hide under here for long. I've got to get help." She wipes her hands clean on her jeans, then reties her pony-tail. She takes a deep breath, then stands up and turns. "Come on."

"Wait!" Big O is still wriggling under the van. I grab his foot and pull him the rest of the way out, then chase after her. She's headed for a stairwell, with me two steps behind. I keep ducking and weaving, scanning the deck for the kidnapper. I have no idea what he looks like, just his shoes, but there's nobody else down here except for us and him.

I've almost caught up to Marissa when I see her flatten herself against the steel-gray wall. She looks back at me and motions with her hand to get down. I drop to the deck and hear Big O do the same. A minute later, Mr. Blank's voice carries over the wind and rattle of the ferry, calling Marissa's name. He's getting closer.

I look around. Not a lot of options here. We could crawl under another car, which might help. Temporarily. Then I notice a steel door set into the wall. It has a big chunky handle on it and a bright yellow sign marked *Crew Only*. I hiss to get Marissa's attention, then start crawling toward the door.

"Marissa?" Mr. Blank is really close now. I reach up and try the latch on the steel door. Marissa and Big O huddle beside me. There's a slight screech as the handle scrapes open and then sticks partway. I freeze. That was pretty loud, but the wind and the creaking of the cars around us might have covered it up. Then Marissa screams and points.

Mr. Blank is running straight for us. He looks like he's just attended a funeral—dress clothes, narrow black tie. And a long black raincoat flapping behind him, like bat wings.

I shove the latch all the way up and swing the door wide open. A puff of moist warm air gusts out of the open door, and I can hear the roar of machinery down below. There's a narrow set of metal stairs leading down into a brightly lit space.

"Go!" Marissa takes the stairs two at a time, followed by Big O. I follow and yank the door shut behind me, seeing Mr. Blank's face contort with anger as it slams closed just before he reaches it. Then I realize there's no latch or lock on this side. He can open the door, no problem. I spin around and hurtle down the stairs.

My shoe catches on something, and I sprawl to one knee.

Looking up, I see the door start to swing open.

I'm on my feet in a flash. I stumble, then jump down the stairs two at a time.

When I reach the bottom, Big O and Marissa are waiting for me. The heat is almost overwhelming. I figure we're in the engine room of the ferry. There are pipes and tubes everywhere, painted in bright primary colors. Huge green metal boxes vibrate—the engines, I guess. The room is arranged in kind of a grid, with four big engines spaced out evenly. Looks like there's no crew down here right now—just machines.

Big O and Marissa seem frozen, not sure where to go. I shove them between two of the vibrating green engines. We slip through to the other side, then start creeping forward. I peek around the corner. No sign of Mr. Blank. Big O taps me on the shoulder.

"We can go back up!" He points at another ladder, leading to a metal catwalk that runs partway around the room.

And at the top is another steel door. A way out, if we're lucky.

I creep to the ladder and look up. Maybe twenty feet of climbing. Not too far, but it will be impossible for Mr. Blank to miss seeing all three of us going up.

Unless he's looking the other way.

I scurry back to Big O and Marissa.

"We need a distraction. Wait a minute before you go up." Big O looks concerned, but I try to be cool and calm. "Not a problem. Piece of cake, bro." I hope he can't see that I really feel like throwing up. That I wish someone else could go and do this. But I don't want to put Marissa or Big O on the line. Before I can think too much about it, I slip around the corner of the thrumming engine. Away from the two of them.

Mr. Blank is walking down the middle of the engine room, right toward me.

Chapter Six

My legs feel rubbery, but I force myself to run right across the open space in front of Mr. Blank. I disappear behind the next massive engine box and turn left, moving fast. I'm hoping he takes the bait and runs after me. Away from the others. Now the trick is to keep him from catching me. Giddily, I think of the games of tag

Big O and I used to play. This is just like that. Catch me if you can.

I dodge to the left again, tuck between two blue pipes, then pop back out into the main space. No sign of Mr. Blank. Now I run back the way we first came, toward the ladder. When my hand closes around a metal rung, I feel relieved—I'm going to make it!

Then I'm in the air and flying sideways into a very hard, round metal tank. My face plants itself right onto a bright-orange triangular sign. I slide to the floor, winded, gasping. I've never played on a football team or anything, but I'm pretty sure that was a really good tackle.

Mr. Blank is standing over me, breathing hard. He has sharp features. Thin nose, dark hair. Intense, focused. Like he's a highly trained specialist. I don't think he specializes in nice things.

His tie is gone. His collar is open. I can see sweat stains under his armpits. He kneels down next to me.

"Where is the girl?" he says slowly and clearly, like he's talking to someone stupid.

I shake my head and shrug.

"You know what your problem is? Not enough motivation. With the right motivation, anything is possible." He swings at me, backhanded. My head snaps back, and fresh pain is added to the mix.

"So there's some motivation for you. Again, where's the girl?"

Mr. Blank looks at me expectantly. But all I can do is sit on the floor and shrug again. I really do not know. Although I'm hoping that Marissa and Big O are very far away by now.

"That's not working for you, huh? Let's try another of my favorite inspirational quotes. This one's from a hockey player, but I think it applies nicely here. *You miss 100 percent of the shots you don't take.*"

Mr. Blank narrows his eyes and pulls a heavy-looking handgun from his raincoat. He points it slowly at me. It gleams flat gray in the fluorescent overhead lights.

I've lost my breath again. The world shrinks down to the muzzle of the gun. I instantly have a really clear picture of how this is going to go down. He shoots me—nobody hears a thing down here in the noisy engine room. He tosses me over the side of the ferry into the middle of the ocean—nobody misses me because there is literally nobody to miss me. Except for Big O.

I really, really don't want to die.

I look around frantically. No crew. Just machines. But then I look straight up, at the orange sign Mr. Blank smashed me into. The one attached to the big metal tank I'm leaning against. A bright-orange triangle with a simplified drawing of an explosion. The words HIGH PRESSURE GAS are stenciled on the tank itself.

I drop my eyes back down to look at Mr. Blank. And I point up at the sign.

His gaze flicks from the sign to me. He gestures to the left with the gun. "So move."

I shake my head. No way. He shoots me, that tank blows up and takes us both with it. That tank is my only protection right now. I slowly stand up, keeping my back pressed against the tank.

Mr. Blank frowns. Waggles the gun again. "Move!"

No.

He rolls his eyes. "Seriously?" he shouts. "Really? This is ridiculous! You realize that I don't need the gun to hurt you, right?" He stuffs the gun back into an inside pocket of his coat. He looks at me and smiles. A mean smile. And starts coming for me.

Something comes flying down from overhead and tinkles onto the floor right in front of him. Mr. Blank looks at the handful of coins that has just landed at his feet. There's another tinkle as more quarters and dimes bounce off the floor.

Then we both look up. Just in time to see Big O leaning over the edge of the stairs with a fire extinguisher. The black nozzle points down at Mr. Blank. There's a sudden stream of white fog that hits him right in the face. Mr. Blank stumbles backward, gasping and rubbing his eyes.

I don't waste any time. I'm up the stairs and out the door, right behind Big O. We run until my chest hurts.

Once we're up on the passenger deck, we try to slow down and look normal. Hard to do when it feels like there's a big red glowing arrow pointed right at me, helpfully pointing out where I am to Mr. Blank. But I do my best.

As we walk by the closed-up gift shop, I say quietly to Big O, "Where'd Marissa go?"

"I don't know. Once we got up that ladder, we were onto the car deck. I told her I was going back for you. That she was on her own."

"You left her alone?" I say. "Think she'll be okay?"

"Are you kidding? She'll be great after she talks to the crew. The crew will give her to the cops, the cops will get her back to her parents and catch the bad guys. It will all be over by the eleven o'clock news. Happy ever after." Then he stops and turns toward me. "And by the way, you're welcome."

"Right," I say. I push him forward again, still looking around for Mr. Blank. "Thank you. Thank you very much. I appreciate it."

"You appreciate it? That's it?" Big O's voice rises. "That's what I get? You know what that guy would've done to you if I hadn't shown up?"

"I had a few ideas. None of them were nice," I say. "And I was going to say thank you. I was just worried about Marissa."

"You appreciate it," Big O mutters. "Next time, maybe I'll let crazy man spend a little more time with you before I save your ass."

"I said, thank you."

"The least you can do is get me something to eat." He points to a bank of vending machines at the end of the passenger section. "I dropped all my change trying to get Mr. Blank to look up at me. And I'm pretty hungry after saving you. Did I mention that you were just rescued by me?"

"I said, thank you!"

We stand in front of a glowing vending machine. I fish around in my pocket, eventually fumbling out some change. You'd think someone who can pick locks would be pretty coordinated, but somehow I manage to drop a quarter on the tile floor. As the ferry shifts in a big wave, the coin slides away and under the machine.

"Damn." I get down on my knees so I can look for the quarter. Gone. As I stand back up, I see something reflected in the shiny front of the vending machine. A familiar figure, a shadowy outline.

Then it clicks.

"That's Mr. Blank," I hiss at Big O. "He's right behind us. Don't turn around."

"Where?" Big O says and starts to look over his shoulder. I shove him so he's facing the vending machine again. In the reflection on the glass, we watch the hazy image of Mr. Blank walk toward us, then turn left and head away. I can't be sure, but I think there's someone right beside him. Someone who looks like Marissa.

Chapter Seven

After a moment, I lean back and look down the corridor. It's definitely her, accompanied by Mr. Blank. He has his arm over her shoulder. Not in a friendly way. They turn again and start down the stairs to the car deck.

"Crap." My stomach goes all cold and tight.

"Guess she didn't make it to the cops after all," says Big O.

"No kidding," I say. I look down at my feet, thinking things through. It's obvious what we need to do, but I don't want to say it out loud.

"You're not going to like this," I say finally. "But I think we need to get some help."

"What do you mean?"

"I mean, tell the crew what's going on. Call the cops ourselves."

Big O leans against the vending machine, shaking his head. "You know we can't do that. I'm in the system. Maybe not right away, but at some point, someone is going to figure out who I am, see my record. That I was charged for assault. Then it's all over."

"I'm clean. I could talk to the cops. Alone," I say.

Big O looks at me hard. "You mean, we split up."

"Yeah. I guess."

"After everything we've been through."

"Just for a little while, then we'd—"

"For this girl, that, that—dammit!" He takes a step back and smacks his palm into the machine. Something jingles inside, and a chocolate bar thumps out of the bottom slot. We both look down, surprised. Big O is thrown for a moment. Then he says, "You can have that. I don't want it."

"No, it's all right. Thanks."

He turns to me. "Will, just take the damn chocolate bar."

I pick it up, split it in half and give him his piece.

"Thanks," Big O says. "You don't even know what the deal is with her."

"Not the biker theory again."

"No, no. I agree with you on that—her shoes are too nice. She's rich." I'm about to interrupt, but he keeps going. "No, I just mean—you do this, then you give up family for a complete stranger. Pretty much the only family you have." Big O punches me in the shoulder. "C'mon. Don't leave me behind. No cops."

I wipe a sweaty hand over my face and check my watch. How long ago did they pass by us? I wonder how much time we have.

"Okay, you're right. We don't go for help," I say. Big O breaks into a huge smile. He reaches out to hug me, and I put a hand on his chest. "But that leaves one other option."

"What?"

"We get her out. Just us. No cops."

Big O lifts his head up, spins around, walks over to a big window. I can't see anything outside in the night, but there's rain and spray tracking across the dark glass. After a minute he turns back to me.

"Well, if that's what it takes. If that's what you want to do. We go get her."

My turn to smile.

"But you'd better really, really appreciate it this time," Big O says.

Chapter Eight

We head down the same stairs that Marissa and Mr. Blank used. I'm assuming he's taken her back to the blue van and locked her up again. Hopefully, nothing more.

"What's the plan?" asks Big O as we step onto the car deck.

"I've got a few ideas."

"That's not very reassuring." We crouch as we get closer to the van, then stop and watch from behind a red sports car. Truth is, I'm actually out of ideas. If this were a movie, it would be simple. We'd go in there, kick open the door and wrestle the bad guy to the ground. In reality, I'm pretty sure that would end badly for us. While I'm thinking, I see the driver's door of the van open, and Mr. Blank steps out. He's talking on a cell phone, one hand pressed against his other ear as he tries to listen. I can just make out what he's saying.

"Again? I can't hear you—the reception is shit. What? I said I will be there at ten. Ten!"

I scuttle forward to the next car so that I can hear him better.

"So call them again, get them to agree. By ten." He shakes his head. "Look, I'm just in charge of delivering her to you. Your job is the negotiation part.

What? Everything is fine here—yeah, no real problems. No, I don't—hello? Hello?" The man looks at the phone, swearing. He disappears into the van, then re-emerges with Marissa. I can't hear what he says to her, but she looks terrified. The man puts his hand firmly on the back of her neck, and together they start walking toward the front of the ferry. He dials with his free hand, then listens. Moves with Marissa and tries again. Finally, he seems to get a clear signal and starts talking again. But he's too far away for me to hear what he says. Anyway, it's time for us to make our move.

"Follow me," I whisper to Big O. We slip around to the side of the van where Mr. Blank can't see us. I kneel next to the front wheel, unscrew the cap on the inflation stem and press one of the tryout keys into it. There's a hiss of air, and the tire gently flattens.

"Ah, so now he can't go anywhere. I get it." Big O shifts from impressed to puzzled. "But wait—how does that help us?"

"I'm not sure," I say. "Just seemed like a good start."

"Excuse me." It's an official-sounding voice coming from behind us. Big O and I slowly stand up and turn around. It's the same crew member from before—Dorkney. Dark-blue coveralls and a bright-orange traffic vest. "Everyone needs to be up above." Then he sees the flat tire. "What's going on?"

"We were just checking this out," I say. "Might cause a problem later on."

The crewman looks concerned. "Yeah, you're right. We'll be docking soon. You got a spare in there?"

"Yes," says Big O. "Nope," I say. We need to get our stories straight.

I forge ahead. "It's not our van. We were just walking by when we saw the flat."

Dorkney thinks this over, studying us. Then there's a flash of recognition.

"Didn't I see the two of you earlier on?" he says.

"Don't think so," I say, but Big O says at the same time, "Yeah, you did!"

I wince.

"We were just walking back to our car. Which is over…" Big O hesitates and looks around. I realize he has no idea where we were the first time Dorkney showed up. And it probably doesn't matter—Dorkney is suspicious enough at this point.

But just then Mr. Blank steps around the front of the van. Marissa is next to him. She sees me and her eyes widen. I have the goofy urge to smile and wave.

"What's going on?" asks Mr. Blank. His cold gaze shifts from Dorkney to Big O to me—and stops on me. I feel a little shaky.

"You've got a flat," says the crewman. "These guys spotted it."

"In fact, we wanted to help fix it," says Big O. *Uh-oh.* Bad things happen when Big O improvises. But Dorkney seems to get into the spirit of things.

"Actually, that might be helpful," Dorkney says. "We're short-staffed. Budget cuts. Just don't tell anyone." He turns to Mr. Blank. "Do you have a spare?"

Mr. Blank looks unimpressed with all the offers of assistance. "I'm fine. I'll take care of it myself."

But Big O is unstoppable. "There's only an hour till we dock. We'd better get going." He starts moving to the rear of the van. "Spare is in the back, right?"

Dorkney, a little flustered, chooses to follow Big O, who starts rattling the rear door.

Mr. Blank takes a couple of steps, as if he's going to stop the two of them. Then he quickly turns back toward Marissa and me. Too late. I've already slipped around so that now I'm between him and the girl. Anger flickers across his face, and he lets his jacket hang open for a moment, revealing the dull gleam of the gun.

"Sir? You mind opening the door? It's locked." It's Dorkney again, popping around the corner of the van. I want to kiss that guy. Mr. Blank can't pull anything nasty with a witness like him around. I think. I hope.

"You know," calls Big O from behind the van, "I think this back tire is looking soft."

"Really?" Dorkney says. He looks worried and disappears again to join Big O.

"What? Just a second," says Mr. Blank. He looks back at me and says quietly, "I don't know what you're doing. But you want to stop right now."

I try to appear innocent—a tough look for me. "I'm just trying to help out a stranger. You had a flat—"

"Don't bullshit me. I don't know who you are or why you keep getting in my way. But it doesn't matter." He leans in close. His dark eyes bore into mine. "Let me give you some advice. You need to know your limits. I know my limits, and they are pretty far out there. Way beyond the normal range of most people. And that makes me very"—he punches a finger into my chest for emphasis—"very good at what I do. So back off and walk away."

"I don't know what you're talking about, trust me—"

"I'm not going to trust you," says Mr. Blank. "I'm just going to hurt you if you do something stupid. Don't do anything stupid. Walk away. The girl doesn't concern you."

"Sir?" It's Dorkney again. Mr. Blank jerks away from me, and the spell is broken. I can move again.

"Sir, we really do need to get this fixed. Don't want a traffic jam when we arrive, do we?" His laugh is somewhere between a snort and a honk. Mr. Blank takes a couple of steps toward him, snarling.

"I get it! I know what the—" I don't hear him finish, because Marissa and I are running across the deck toward the end of the ferry.

Chapter Nine

I'd like to say I ran because I was brave. Because I wanted to defy Mr. Blank and save Marissa. But in that moment, I just panicked. I wanted to get the hell away from that scary freak. I grabbed Marissa's hand, and off we went.

But we literally run out of room—pretty fast. The end of the car deck is partly open, with rain and spray coming in sideways out of the dark. I look back and see Mr. Blank stalking down the alley between the cars. The worst thing is that he's not rushing. He knows we're stuck. I can partly see Dorkney way behind him, lying flat out on the deck beside the van. Knocked out. Or worse.

And Big O is nowhere to be seen.

I put my hands on the metal gate that forms the edge of the deck. I can't see anything out there with the rain and wind. No way to climb up or down. We can run between the cars if we go left or right. But Mr. Blank will see us, and at the narrow end of the ferry, there just isn't a lot of maneuvering room.

"He's getting really close," says Marissa.

"I get that," I say. "I do." I keep scanning the deck, looking for a way out.

Finally, I have an idea. I yank the tryout keys from my pocket and start working on the little compact car right

next to us. I send up a silent prayer—
*please let me open this car on the first
attempt.* And it works. There's a solid
clunk as the lock disengages.

Now Mr. Blank starts running at us.

"In!" I open the door and shove
Marissa inside, then clamber in behind
her. Mr. Blank is right there, so close
that he grabs the edge of the door frame,
reaching in for me.

That's when I slam the door shut—
as hard as I can.

There's a crunching sound as it
closes.

Then a muffled scream from
Mr. Blank.

"Go! GO!" I shout at Marissa,
pushing her out the door on the other
side of the car. I sneak a quick look back
as we run toward a stairwell. Mr. Blank
is leaning on the hood of the little car,
cradling his right hand. Judging from the

sound, I'd say most of the fingers must be broken. I've never hurt someone like that in my life, but he totally deserved it. Big O will be impressed. He's normally the heavy hitter.

That's when it hits me.

"Where's Big O?"

"Who?" says Marissa.

"My brother. I didn't see him back there." The crew member, Dorkney, was lying on the deck the last time I looked, knocked down by Mr. Blank. But what happened to Big O?

"We can't stop now." Marissa pulls on my hand. "Let's find somewhere safe, get some help. Then we'll find him."

"No. He came back for me when I was in trouble. He always does. I gotta go back."

Marissa grabs my shoulders and makes me look straight at her. "You go back right now, and that man will stomp all over you. Be smart." The deep blue of her eyes slows me down, calms me. "Your brother wouldn't want that, right?"

So I follow her, thinking that Big O has got to be okay. Because if I start thinking about any of the other options, I'm not going to be able to keep it together.

Breathing hard, we reach the top of the stairs. We are in a section near the front of the ferry. Rows and rows of padded seats are occupied by travelers of various types. Families with sleeping babies or screaming toddlers. Old folks doing crosswords. A bunch of teenage guys in hockey jerseys. Marissa and I slip through the crowd, her in the lead. But I pull her to a stop as we walk by a darkened room—an arcade occupied by a few aging video games but otherwise empty.

"In here." We step into the dimly lit room and sit down in the twin seats of a driving game. We're both facing forward, looking at an identical view of a car screaming through a digital landscape. Big flashing letters scroll sideways across the screen—*OUTRUNNER! Insert Coins to Play!*

"I don't think he'll see us in here." I need to take a second. Figure things out. I realize my hands are shaking. I put them on the fake steering wheel in front of me.

"I thought we were going to get help," Marissa says. She looks dubiously at me, lit by the glow from the screens in front of us. "You okay?"

I'm not okay. The adrenaline is draining out of my system, leaving me feeling shaky and freaked out. I want her to understand, to explain things clearly. But it all comes out in babbling rush. "We can't get help from anyone. See, Big O had this plan—but then things got really complicated, really fast. The plan was—we stole some money. From the cars on the ferry. But then we found you." I can't help it, but I even start to tear up. "We just needed a hundred bucks."

"You guys were breaking into cars down there?" says Marissa. She leans her head back against the seat, then looks at me again. "That's how you found me? You were robbing the van?"

She actually starts to laugh.

"What?" I wipe at my eye with my sleeve, hoping she doesn't notice.

"I just—I thought you somehow heard me down there and ripped open the door. Saved me like a superhero." She smiles sadly. "But you just wanted to steal Mr. Blank's spare change and accidentally found me?"

"Basically." I nod. "Big O wanted some new CDs too."

She laughs again and rubs the bridge of her nose. "What's the *O* stand for, anyway?"

"Orville. Our dad was really into planes and stuff. Named us after the guys who invented the first airplane. Wilbur and Orville Wright."

Marissa looks at me and raises an eyebrow. "Wilbur and Orville." She shakes her head. "Doesn't sound right for a pair of superheroes."

"Yeah." I shrug. "We're no heroes."

"Either way, I guess, you still saved me," she says. "So you're Wilbur."

"Everyone calls me Will."

We stare at each other for a moment in the flickering light of the video game. She's really pretty. Not like a doll or someone from a fashion magazine. But pretty in a real-person kind of way. I like how she smiles. A little shy, a little guarded. Like maybe there's more waiting for you.

"Nice to meet you, Will," she says finally.

Chapter Ten

My hands feel a little steadier now, resting on the pretend steering wheel.

"Okay, I need to get back out there. Find Big O." I get up from the seat and stretch carefully. I'm aching in a whole bunch of places. I probe my jaw tenderly. My face still hurts from where Mr. Blank hit me. Marissa stands up too, and we step out of the dim arcade and into the brightly lit corridor. A young woman pushes an old grandma in a wheelchair past us.

"Look, like I said, I can't go with you to the crew or the cops," I say quietly. "But you should go get help."

"I should." But she doesn't move. Just keeps staring over my shoulder, watching. "The thing is, last time I went off on my own, Mr. Blank showed up. It's like he's unstoppable. I mean, what if the crew can't protect me?"

"Marissa, you're so close to being safe," I say, taking a step toward her, studying her face. "Don't be scared. Just find someone from the crew. Anyone."

"Dorkney," she says.

"Well, maybe not him," I say. "He seems a bit clueless."

"No, I mean Dorkney is right there." Sure enough, I look over my shoulder to see Dorkney coming down the corridor, waving his arms and talking with two other men in blue uniforms. He has a big bruise around one eye. Marissa grabs my hand and spins us around. We stay in front of them, walking fast in the same direction.

"Wait—I was kidding," I say quietly as we walk. "You can talk to him."

"But you shouldn't, right?" She looks at me quickly. "They'll keep you for questioning, maybe hold you until we dock. After what you've done for me, the least I can do is make sure you can find your brother." We've come to an intersection where two corridors meet. I hesitate, but Marissa doesn't. She shoves me to the left, toward a door to the outer deck. She pushes down on the handle, and the wind outside yanks the door open.

The storm is brutal, wind hammering against us as we push the door shut. Just in time too. We watch through the glass window in the door as Dorkney and the other crew members stop at the intersection, talking. We wait for them to move. In seconds, we're soaked. Cold, wet and shivering. I can hear the waves slamming against the hull far below us.

Enough of this. I'm not waiting around for Dorkney to move. There's got to be another door up ahead. One hand on the wall, the other grasping Marissa's hand, I haltingly move forward. We stumble across the deck. It's cold enough that some of the rain is turning to slush. Combined with the rolling of the ferry and my crappy shoes, it's tricky just to stay upright.

We reach a lifeboat station—a metal cage containing a big orange pill-shaped container. It stops the wind just enough to let us rest behind it for a moment.

"Maybe we should go back," yells Marissa over the wind. Her ponytail has fallen out, and her blond hair is plastered to her head. She shivers.

"No. Just a little farther," I say. Dorkney might still be there. We leave the shelter of the lifeboat station and keep pushing on into the wind. I squint through the rain and see a door up ahead. It's at the end of the passenger section. Beyond that, there's a waist-high white metal railing that separates this area from a forward part of the deck.

I break into a half-run. Stupid. Almost immediately, I lose my footing and slip to the deck. I'm wobbling back upright when there's a sudden, juddering impact. I feel the vibration through the hull of the ferry beneath me. The ferry rises, then comes down really fast as we pass through a massive wave. Too much for my lousy balance to handle. I stumble and slide forward. Toward the white metal railing. Fast.

The railing hits me in the stomach. Off balance, I flip right over it and land on my back. Now I'm sliding down the slush-slick deck, the breath knocked out of me.

I've fallen into the forward area of the deck—the part that's off-limits to passengers. The ferry begins to rise up again on the next wave. My slide finally slows, and I come to a stop against a big round tower wrapped in thick metal cable, like a spool of thread for a giant. Instinctively, I reach down to my ankle. There's a sharp pain deep inside it— something twisted when I slipped, and it isn't good. I wipe my other hand across my eyes to clear the rain from them, then look back.

Marissa is climbing over the white railing. Coming to get me. The ferry starts another carnival ride, rising toward the top of the next wave. But Marissa is too smart to fall. She takes it slow, staying on her hands and knees. Crawling until she reaches my side. She sees me holding my ankle.

"You okay?" she yells.

I shake my head. "Hurts." The wind rips the words out of my mouth.

"Lean on me."

Again, I shake my head. No way—we try that, and I suspect we might slip right over the side of the boat and into the dark ocean below. I look through the rain, trying to see a little more of where we are. It's the very front of the ferry. There's a wide span of flat steel that forms the deck, punctuated by a few of the giant spools of cable. I start to shiver hard, my body feeling colder than ever before. The passenger section on this level ends here. Above us is the bridge, a row of dark windows topped with spinning radar towers and antennae. The crew probably can't see us down here, right underneath them. They definitely couldn't hear us over the storm, even if we shouted. So it's up to us to figure a way out.

Then Marissa spots something. She shakes my shoulder and points. Maybe half a dozen feet away is a small metal hatch set into the wall beneath the bridge windows. It must lead back inside.

"Can you crawl?" she asks. In answer, I roll over and start pulling myself across the deck with my arms. The ferry starts another plunge downward to the bottom of a wave. I lie flat during the worst part, then keep moving. It only takes a few moments, but it feels like hours as I drag myself over the cold deck. Finally, Marissa and I lean against the wall next to the hatch. Now to get inside and get dry.

Except the hatch is locked.

Chapter Eleven

Marissa tries to open it, again and again. Doesn't budge. She looks over at me, water streaming down her face. Panicking. I reach out to her with an open hand.

"Help me up. Need to get closer." She gets one shoulder under mine and lifts me up until I'm almost standing. I examine the lock as carefully as I can.

Okay, maybe I can do this. I reach into the inside pocket of my jacket. Not the slim jim, not the tryout keys. There—a little leather pouch containing a bunch of thin metal tools. My lockpicks. Stole them from my dad years ago, and I've gotten pretty good with them. Just hope they do the trick this time around.

Keeping a firm grip on the little pouch, I carefully open it and select a pair of picks. A thin, strong tension bar and another with a hook on the end. It looks like something a dentist would use. Leaning against the hatch, I slip the tools into the lock. I try to focus through the gusts of wind and rain. Try to steady the shake in my hands. I close my eyes and start working the tools around. After a minute, I twist too hard and one of the picks slips out. In the rain and dark, I can't see where it went. I drop to the deck and feel around for the pick, ignoring the pain in my ankle. Finally, my fingers close around the thin piece of metal. Slowly, I stand back up and look at Marissa. Her arms are crossed tightly across her thin sweater, trying to keep warm. She looks so cold and wet.

"We should try something else," I shout. "I don't think I can do this."

"Yes, you can," she says and smiles weakly. "Try again."

I put the picks in, shut my eyes and close everything out. The storm. Mr. Blank. Big O and Marissa. I push all of it away until my entire universe consists only of the lockpicks and the lock. I start to work, pushing down with one pick and raking the other across the pins hidden inside the lock. Carefully, painstakingly. Pushing and holding each pin up until I can twist the tension bar and the pick together.

And the lock gives way with a click I can't hear over the storm but can feel in my fingers.

I shove my picks back into my jacket pocket. Working together, Marissa and I haul open the hatch. Once the hatch is closed behind us, I look around. We're in some sort of storage locker for the crew. It's dimly lit and filled with ropes and cables. Not the fuzzy blankets and hot coffee I was hoping for. But I smile when I see another door at the opposite end.

"Maybe that'll get us back inside," I say, my voice hoarse after all the shouting. I lurch toward it, holding on to the metal shelves around me for support. I realize I can barely walk at all, my ankle hurts so much.

"Wait," says Marissa. She reaches across one of the shelves and pulls out a red plastic box with a white cross on it. "You can't go anywhere. We need to take care of your leg first. Sit." Part of me wants to get out of here and to somewhere really warm and dry. But she's right. Something is really messed up in my ankle. I slide gingerly to the floor. Marissa pops open the medical kit.

"Hey!" she says happily. She pulls out a couple of small foil packages. "Heat blankets!" She unwraps them, thin pieces of foil about the size of a bedsheet. She wraps one blanket around herself and tucks the other around my shoulders. Then she rolls up the soaked cuff of my jeans.

"Does that hurt?" she asks, carefully prodding and poking my swollen ankle.

I jerk my leg back from the flash of pain.

"Stop that!" I say. "Do you know what you're doing?"

Marissa looks at me, a little pissed. "Actually, I do. I'm a lifeguard at our pool. I've dealt with a few owies. Most kids are a little braver than you though." She pokes a little more. "I think it's a sprain." Taking out a roll of tensor bandage, she sets to work wrapping up my ankle. "Man up—no whining, okay?"

I grunt. What's a little more pain today?

"That was pretty impressive with the lock," she says while she works. "Where'd you learn to do that?"

"My dad, mostly. He's kind of an expert."

"So stealing things runs in your family, huh?" Marissa asks.

"Yeah. My dad is more of a high-end burglar. He was, I mean. Not anymore. When he gets out of jail, he's going to get out of the business."

"You dad was caught?"

"Actually, he kind of killed a guy."

Marissa stops short, holding the brown bandage in midair. She looks at me for a moment. "How do you *kind of* kill a guy?"

"It's not what you think," I say quickly. "Dad had just finished a job, robbing this fancy apartment. He actually had his hand on the doorknob to leave when this old guy opened it from the other side. It was the owner. Dad tried to talk his way out of it. But then he smiled at him. Honestly, Dad's smile is spooky at the best of times. Bad teeth."

Marissa laughs and starts wrapping the bandage around my leg.

"Anyway, for whatever reason, the old guy seized up and had a heart attack. Right there in front of Dad. Now, Dad is a thief, but he's not a murderer. He wasn't going to take off with this guy dying in front of him."

"So what'd he do?" asks Marissa.

"Dad performed CPR while a neighbor called nine-one-one. And that's how the cops found my dad—pockets full of stolen jewels and cash, pounding away on the old guy's chest. Hey, that feels better." I test the tightly wrapped ankle. Marissa smiles and closes up the box.

"What about your mom?"

"Mom left the picture years ago. So my brother and I were packed up and delivered to a group home for some proper supervision. Except that didn't work out so well. About a month ago, another kid went after me. Big O hit him back—knocked him out. Then we took off. Figured Big O might be charged with assault."

"Where did you go?"

"Nowhere. Stealing enough to get by, sleeping in our pickup. Until last week. That's when I convinced Big O we should head over to our uncle's place in Seattle. We don't really know him that well, but Dad always said he was a good guy. The honest one in the family. We figured we could stay with him for a little while, anyway. Maybe get a real job. Man, I'd love to go back to school again."

Marissa looks at me like I'm crazy.

"No, seriously," I say. "I'd like that. Sitting at a desk all day again. Learning history. Math formulas. It sounds—safe. You know?"

"I do," she says. "Guess I always kind of took *safe* for granted. It looks a lot like boring sometimes."

I nod, then test my ankle. Not too bad. "Speaking of being safe, I need to get out of here and find Big O. You dried off?"

Marissa shrugs and tries to pull her hair back into a ponytail. "I feel like a wet sponge. How do I look?"

I study her perfect face and deep-blue eyes. My brain locks for a second. "You look nice," I say finally.

She snorts. "That's sweet, but bullshit." We take a second to ditch the heat blankets and straighten up our clothes. Then we open the inner hatch and step into the hallway.

Chapter Twelve

We're in the clear. No Dorkney, no Mr. Blank. Just a pair of teenagers leaning against the wall, trying to sleep against their backpacks despite the rocking of the ferry in the storm. I stumble as I lead Marissa over to a map of the ferry on the wall. It takes me a moment to figure out where we are. Upper deck, close to the cafeteria.

"So where do you want to start?" asks Marissa, studying the map.

"If Big O is hurt, my guess is he's still at Mr. Blank's van. Or chucked over the side of the ferry, if—"

"Slow down," interrupts Marissa. "Let's assume he got away. He's a smart guy. Where would he go?"

I think, spinning slowly on one foot. The fried-food smell from the cafeteria makes my stomach grumble. "Hang on. I just remembered. Before this all started, I think I told him to meet me in the cafeteria if we got split up."

"Okay, we'll start there." She starts marching down the hallway. I don't move.

"Wait," I say. "We?"

She looks back over her shoulder. "Just for a little longer, okay? Like I said, I owe you. But I'm going after we find your brother at the cafeteria."

She's sounds so sure of herself, I'm not arguing. I follow.

It turns out the cafeteria is shut down. A big sign on the wall reads *Cafeteria closes thirty minutes prior to arrival.* There are still one or two people sitting at the square plastic tables. A guy in a suit, tapping away on a laptop, and a gray-haired woman asleep in a chair, paperback open on her chest.

"What's that?" says Marissa. She points at a table empty except for a baseball cap. An Oakland A's cap. I hurriedly weave in between the tables. Sure enough, it's the one that Big O always wears. And there is a note beneath it, in Big O's spidery handwriting.

Meet me in the kitchen.

I look around and see the steel door that leads into the kitchen. There's an official-looking sign on it that says *Closed.* Without thinking, I start toward it. Looking around to make sure no one is watching, I push gently on the door. It's unlocked. I shove it all the way open and step inside.

There are only a few lights on in here, sparkling off the stainless-steel counters and pots. Deep shadows hide the corners of the room. I take a few steps in.

"Big O?" I whisper. Something moves in the dark, over near the sink. "You in here?"

"Yeah, Orville is here," says Mr. Blank. He steps out of the shadows, shoving Big O ahead of him. "He told me about your plan to meet up in the cafeteria. It took a little convincing, mind you." Big O is limping a little. He winces as Mr. Blank shoves the gun into his side. His hands are bound together in front of him with duct tape, and his mouth is covered with it too.

"You all right?" I ask him. Big O nods, but he looks scared. Big O never looks scared. "Listen, it's all going to be okay—"

"Shut up," says Mr. Blank. He moves behind me and locks the door I just walked through. He turns to me and points the gun. "Empty your pockets. Slowly." I swallow, then drop my wallet, the tryout keys and the lockpick set onto the counter. He looks quickly through the wallet.

"You're Wilbur, huh? Your brother said you were crooks." He sees the handful of bills—all the money we stole earlier. "Not very successful ones, apparently." He pockets my wallet.

Damn. Losing all our money is the least of my worries right now, but it still sucks.

Mr. Blank turns his attention back to me. "So, Wilbur, where's the girl?"

I look around, expecting to see Marissa. She's gone. Confused, I turn slowly back to Mr. Blank and shrug.

"You don't know where she is?" he says. "That's what you said last time."

"She was behind me a second ago," I say apologetically.

Mr. Blank's face clenches angrily, eyes squinting.

"What is it with you? This was supposed to be a simple job," he says. "I'm a professional, and I really like simplicity. I like a clean job. But you two"—he waves the gun at Big O and me, voice rising—"you came out of nowhere and screwed it all up!"

He sighs heavily a couple of times, sniffs, pulls himself together.

"This can work. What does not kill me makes me stronger." He quickly swings the gun straight at me. "You know who said that?"

I try to swallow, but my throat is suddenly dry and sandy. I just shake my head.

"Nietzsche. Great philosopher. Punk like you probably never even heard of him." Still keeping the gun trained on me, Mr. Blank moves closer to me. Close enough that I can smell a mix of sweat and sickly sweet cologne. "You need to educate yourself." With the butt of the gun, he smacks my head. I stumble.

Big O takes a step forward, grunting. Mr. Blank swings the gun back to him. "Uh-uh. You don't want to do that. Just watch." He turns back to me. "Today's lesson is this. The secret of success is learning how to use pain and pleasure instead of having pain and pleasure use you."

He looks satisfied with himself. I try to look interested and not just terrified.

"Know who said that?" Mr. Blank says.

I answer quietly, "Nietzsche?"

"No!" I can't help flinching when he raises his voice. "No, that's Tony Robbins. Wise man. The point is, I know how to use pain particularly well. I am also currently in great pain because of what you did." He raises his right hand, swollen and purple. He scans a row of kitchen utensils in a rack on the wall. "So I am going to use that pain to help teach you a lesson. Which will give me pleasure." Shoving the gun back into his raincoat, he picks out a heavy meat tenderizer—a hammer with nasty ridges on both sides.

"Wilbur, when I'm done," he says, "you're going to tell me where the girl is. And I'm going to get on with my job. And you will not interfere again."

Mr. Blank gestures with the meat tenderizer. "Put your hands on the counter. Spread them out."

I look over Mr. Blank's shoulder at Big O. He stares at me helplessly over the duct tape across his mouth. Then I see Marissa rise up beside Big O, emerging from the shadows like a ghost. I try not to let my expression change.

I need to keep Mr. Blank's attention, so I slowly do what he says. I put my palms down on the cool surface of the metal countertop. Behind Mr. Blank, I see Marissa cutting Big O's hands free with a kitchen knife.

"Now, only one of my hands was crushed," mutters Mr. Blank. "You can tell me what two smashed hands feels like, tough guy." He firmly holds one of my wrists and, with his other hand, raises the hammer. Ready to smash it down on my splayed fingers. I close my eyes.

"Wait!" I yell. "I'll tell you where she is!" I don't feel any pain, so I open one eye and cautiously look at Mr. Blank. He's still ready with the hammer.

"I told her to wait for me by our truck," I say. "That we'd get her off the ferry."

Mr. Blank pushes in close to my face and looks in my eyes.

"You expect me to believe that?" Mr. Blank says. The hammer swings down, smashing into the counter with a metallic crash. I yelp.

But there's no pain. I look down at the big dent on the counter where the meat tenderizer crashed into it. Mr. Blank lifts the hammer back into the air, ready to swing again.

"One. More. Try. This time, the truth. Where's the—" he begins but is interrupted by a loud voice from a speaker mounted in the ceiling. It sounds like someone speaking through a toilet-paper tube, with extra fuzz on top.

"This is a passenger announcement," the speaker rasps. "As we are nearing our destination, all drivers should return to their vehicles now."

Mr. Blank squints angrily and takes a deep shuddering breath. Trying to stay cool.

"This is not working out the way I planned. Okay, fine. Let's speed this up. Where's the girl?" he yells.

"Right here," says Marissa quietly from behind him. Mr. Blank spins around in surprise, right into the cast-iron frying pan that Big O is swinging like a baseball bat at him. There's a crunch as the pan lands somewhere between his shoulder and neck. Mr. Blank drops in a crumpled heap to the floor. For a second, we all just stare at the gently breathing body on the floor.

"Wow," I say. "That was a ten out of ten."

"Maybe I'll make it to the Olympics, coach," says Big O. "You got anything to say to me?"

"Thank you," I say. "Thank you for saving me. Again." I wrap my arms around him in a bear hug, and he shrugs me off.

"No big deal. Gotta take care of family."

"You guys done?" asks Marissa. "Can we go?"

Mr. Blank groans on the floor. Big O and I nod and head for the door. I freeze when I see the handle turning by itself. Someone is coming in from the other side.

I grab Big O and head in the opposite direction as fast as I can. There's another way out—a white swinging door at the other end of the kitchen. I'm not sure where it leads, but at this point it doesn't matter. Big O goes through first, and I'm about to follow when I look back over my shoulder at Marissa. She hasn't moved—she's just standing next to the unconscious form of Mr. Blank.

"You coming?" I say.

She shakes her head, smiling sadly. "Go. Run. I have to stay," she says.

I don't want to move, but Big O drags me back through the swinging door. We're in a dark storage cupboard that's like a small hallway with racks of cans and plastic buckets lining the walls. I start to move toward the other end, where there's an exit. But I suddenly stop when I hear Dorkney's voice, muffled by the door to the kitchen. I can't make out what he's saying. But then I hear Marissa—clearly.

"Two guys? No, there wasn't anyone else," she says. "I'm lucky I escaped on my own."

Chapter Thirteen

The next door leads into a main corridor, and we mix in with the crowd heading to the lower decks. A few minutes later, we're back in the pickup truck. Right where we started. Big O looks in the rearview mirror, delicately touching a bruise on his cheek. I loosen the bandage around my ankle a little. It still hurts like hell. We're a mess.

"You know," I say, "I have a new rule."

"Why am I not surprised?" says Big O.

"Here it is. You are never, ever allowed to come up with the plan. Only me."

Red taillights flare ahead of us, and the engines of the cars surrounding us rumble to life. Big O turns the key in the ignition. Our pickup coughs twice, then starts.

"Really? I thought my plan worked out pretty well," Big O says. "At least we made our hundred bucks."

"Ah, you are wrong again," I say. "Mr. Blank emptied my pockets, remember? He took it all. We've got no money. I lost my tools. Nothing but bruises and aches to show for your plan."

Big O stares at me. The car behind us honks, and that snaps him back to reality. He shifts the truck into Drive and inches it forward toward the exit ramp.

"In that case," he says, "I can see your point. You make the plans from now on."

We rumble over the ramp and down to the road. In the distance, I can see flashing red-and-blue lights. A line of cop cars coming down the highway toward the ferry terminal. For a moment, I have a vision of a roadblock, of an officer asking me questions I don't want to answer. But we drive right by and out onto the open road. The pale light of dawn is starting to wash over the sky. We pick up speed as we hit the highway.

"Could've been worse," says Big O after a while. "We helped Marissa. Instead of being bad guys, we got to be heroes for a moment."

"Yeah," I say. "That felt pretty good. Maybe you should plan on sticking with being a hero." Big O looks at me to see if I'm joking. "After all," I say, "you're kind of useless at the whole criminal thing."

Big O reaches over and punches my shoulder, laughing. I'm not sure how we're going to get to our uncle's, or what is going to happen to us after that. But it feels like we've finally left the bad stuff behind. That maybe we've escaped.

DATE DUE

Se
an
ey
of
fo
at
Sn
tau
ath
stu
co
sc
Vi
in